TAKING IT
TO THE MAT

BY JAKE MADDOX

text by
Peter Mavrikis

STONE ARCH BOOKS
a capstone imprint

Published by Stone Arch Books, an imprint of Capstone
1710 Roe Crest Drive, North Mankato, Minnesota 56003
capstonepub.com

Library of Congress Cataloging-in-Publication Data
Names: Maddox, Jake, author. | Mavrikis, Peter, author. | Maddox, Jake. Jake Maddox JV.
Title: Taking it to the mat / [Jake Maddox ; text] by Peter Mavrikis.
Description: North Mankato, MN : Stone Arch Books, an imprint of Capstone, 2022. |
Series: Jake Maddox JV | Audience: Ages 9–12. | Audience: Grades 4–6. | Summary:
Fourteen-year-old Aarash Husayni is starting his freshman year at Freemont Central High
School, and even though he has been in the United States for six years, he still feels like
an outsider. He mostly he tries to keep his head down and avoid the bullies. So when his
fifteen-year-old cousin, Ferhana, and her friend Anton persuade him to join the wrestling
team, it is a big step—but his chief tormentor is also on the team, and Aarash has a choice:
quit the team, or face down the bully.
Identifiers: LCCN 2021012642 (print) | LCCN 2021012643 (ebook) | ISBN 9781663920386
(paperback) | ISBN 9781663910950 (hardcover) | ISBN 9781663910929 (ebook pdf)
Subjects: LCSH: Afghan Americans—Juvenile fiction. | Wrestling—Juvenile fiction. |
Bullying—Juvenile fiction. | Self-confidence—Juvenile fiction. | CYAC: Afghan
Americans—Fiction. | Wrestling—Fiction. | Bullying—Fiction. | Self-confidence—Fiction.
Classification: LCC PZ7.M25643 Tan 2021 (print) | LCC PZ7.M25643 (ebook) | DDC 813.6
[Fic]—dc23
LC record available at https://lccn.loc.gov/2021012642
LC ebook record available at https://lccn.loc.gov/2021012643

Editorial Credits
Editor: Alison Deering; Designer: Bobbie Nuytten; Media Researcher: Jo Miller;
Production Specialist: Tori Abraham

Image Credits
Shutterstock: Ahturner, 5 and throughout, JoeSAPhotos, cover, back cover, sportoakimirka,
1 and throughout

Design Elements: Shutterstock

Thank you to Derek Brophy, Kathleen Ganteaume-Brophy, and Michele Mavrikis
for all their help throughout the writing of this book.

TABLE OF CONTENTS

CHAPTER I

YESTERDAY'S MEATLOAF

Aarash Husayni tucked the change in his pocket, politely thanked the cafeteria worker, and stepped into the lunchroom. The room was flooded with the noise of more than a hundred chatting students.

So many new faces, Aarash thought, scanning the tables. Even though it was his second week at Freemont Central High School, he remained lost in the crowd.

Finally he spotted his cousin, Ferhana, sitting in the back of the cafeteria. At fifteen years old, she was a sophomore and one year older than Aarash. She was eating lunch with her friend Anton and a few other students Aarash didn't know.

Ferhana waved to Aarash and pointed to a vacant seat next to her. It was the only empty chair left at the crowded table. It was clear she had saved it for him.

Aarash waved back. He appreciated Ferhana looking out for him, but he wished he had his own friends and wasn't such a tagalong. Still, he knew he was lucky to have her.

Ferhana was more of a sister than a cousin. She and Aarash had lived together ever since Aarash's father was killed in a car accident six years ago. It had happened when Aarash was eight years old, just a few months after he and his father had come to the United States from Afghanistan.

"Come on, slow poke!" Ferhana said as Aarash approached. She moved her books off of the chair and motioned for Aarash to sit. "What took you so long?"

"Maybe he had a tough time deciding on whether to go for the sloppy joe," Anton added with a smile. "You know that's just yesterday's meatloaf, right, Aarash?"

Aarash cracked a smile and sat down.

"So?" Ferhana nudged her cousin. "How's it going this week? Freemont Central is ten times the size of your old school. Are you still wandering the halls and getting lost?"

"I'm good," Aarash answered. "The dozen maps that you drew for me on your dad's restaurant napkins have helped. You better hope he doesn't find out how you waste them," he added with a slight smile. "I already used a couple of them to blow my nose this morning."

Anton laughed. "You're funny, Aarash. You know, if you showed people that part of your personality, you'd be making friends in no time." He paused. "How's that coming along?"

"Still working on it," Aarash answered as a spitball suddenly hit his check. He quickly wiped it away, hoping nobody noticed, but it was too late. Ferhana and Anton caught sight of the action.

Aarash looked around to see where it had come from, but he had a feeling he already knew the culprit. It was clear when he spotted two boys snickering a few tables away.

Ferhana's face flushed with concern. Before she could do anything, Aarash placed his hand on her shoulder.

"Don't," he said. "I can't have my cousin sticking up for me. Besides, if they know it bothers me they'll just do it more."

"That's messed up," Anton muttered, staring at the boys at the other table. "Who are those guys? Obviously freshmen, but still . . . very uncool. I'll dump this tray of yesterday's meatloaf all over their heads if you want me to."

"I appreciate the offer," Aarash replied as he ran his fork through his food. "The blond kid is in my biology class. His name is Shane, and he's taken a liking to calling me 'A-Rash.' I don't know the other mouth breather next to him. Not yet at least."

"I knew jerks like that when I was a freshman, but they never messed with me. Especially after I started wrestling." Anton grinned. "I mean, don't get me wrong, I love playing football and being part of the team, but wrestling is what gave me the confidence to deal with creeps like that."

"Yeah, well, that's great, but I would never make it through tryouts," Aarash said. Although he and Anton were about the same height, Aarash weighed at least thirty pounds less. He also lacked Anton's muscular build.

"Not sure if you realized," Aarash added, "but I'm not exactly wrestling material." He bent his right arm in a comical attempt to make a muscle. Anton and Ferhana laughed.

"Put your arm down. You might scare those two," Ferhana added. She nodded toward the two bullies, who seemed to have lost interest in Aarash.

"I have good news for you," Anton said. "Wrestling doesn't have tryouts! Just work hard, show you're committed, and learn. That's all Coach Beckett asks for."

"I'll think about it," Aarash said half-heartedly. He watched as Shane and the other boy got up from their table and left the cafeteria. "It would be nice to be able to stand up to them. . . ."

"You should do it, cuz. Look at Anton," Ferhana said. "Before he joined the wrestling team two years ago, I was his only friend."

"Yeah, you wish!" Anton answered. "But seriously, man. Come with me to the first team meeting. It's this week. What do you have to lose?"

"Yes, please. . . ." Ferhana pleaded with her cousin. She tugged on Aarash's arm. "You'll like it. It beats running to the restaurant after school and helping my father."

"It'll give you confidence, add some muscle to your frame, and help you make friends," Anton added. "And don't believe Ferhana. I had plenty of friends even before joining wrestling."

"I bet," Aarash added. He still felt embarrassed and wondered if anyone else in the cafeteria had seen him get hit by the spitball. "Okay, maybe. . . ."

"I'm going to take that 'maybe' as a yes," Anton responded cheerfully.

"Fine," Aarash agreed. "I'll do it. I'll go with you." After all, as Anton had said, what did he have to lose?

CHAPTER 2

A FAMILY LEGACY

Aarash pumped the spray bottle one final time and ran the damp cloth over the last table in the restaurant's main dining room. It was a little past ten o'clock on a Thursday evening—a school night—but Uncle Babak was shorthanded this evening, and Aarash didn't mind helping.

Aarash was used to spending a lot of time at Babak's Kebab and Grill. He had been helping Uncle Babak and Aunt Emily at the restaurant since he'd moved in with them. He biked to the restaurant right after school and usually finished his schoolwork in his uncle's office soon after he arrived.

Aarash thought about his classes as he worked. For the most part, Freemont Central was a great school, with the exception of Shane Tasovac. Shane had homed in on Aarash from day one. It had started in biology class and continued throughout the day— in English class, walking down the halls, and now even in the lunchroom.

Avoiding Shane wasn't much help either. For whatever reason, Shane had it in for him. And their run-ins—and Aarash's problems—seemed to be multiplying.

"What are you daydreaming about?" Uncle Babak asked from the other side of the dining area. He pushed the wooden chairs against the tables. "Are you tired? I'm sorry for keeping you here so late. We will go home soon."

"No," Aarash said as he turned to help his uncle move the remaining chairs. "Just thinking, I guess."

Aarash paused. Uncle Babak was the closest family he had. Sometimes it felt like he was the only person Aarash could talk to, especially since the death of his father. It helped that Babak, who had moved to the United States twenty years earlier to attend college, also knew Pashto. It was the language Aarash had spoken in Afghanistan.

Luckily, it hadn't taken long for Aarash to learn English. That was mostly thanks to Aunt Emily, who had been a third-grade teacher. It also helped that Uncle Babak had paid for private tutors and enrolled Aarash in a small private school in Freemont to start.

"Well?" his uncle asked. "Are you going to tell me what you're thinking about or not? Or perhaps you want me to guess?"

"Sure," Aarash responded with a smile. "Give it a shot and take a guess."

"What will I get if I guess right?" his uncle asked. "Will you help me with this weekend's stew? I'm thinking pumpkin and lentil."

"Deal," Aarash responded. "Now guess."

"Are you thinking about joining the wrestling team?" Uncle Babak asked.

Aarash was surprised—and a little irritated. "How did you know about that?" he asked, frowning. "Did Ferhana tell you?"

Uncle Babak moved toward the bar, pulled out a stool, and took a seat. He motioned for Aarash to sit next to him.

"Don't be angry with your cousin," Uncle Babak said. "She told me because she was excited for you. Truth is, when Ferhana told me about the wrestling, it reminded me of when I was in high school in Kabul. Your father was also a part of the wrestling team."

What? Aarash was surprised to hear this piece of family history. He'd never known his father was a wrestler. Nobody ever talked about it.

Uncle Babak continued. "It was during what we will call *less* troubled times. When life was as normal as I could remember. Your father liked the sport, he loved school, and he was the best English-speaker in the family. He was three years younger, but he was even better than me."

Aarash smiled. That part wasn't a total surprise. He knew it was thanks to his father's skills and work as a translator for the U.S. military that Aarash was living in America today.

"I never knew this about my father," Aarash said. "The wrestling part, I mean. What happened?"

"The Taliban took over," Babak said. Aarash could see the pain and sadness in his uncle's eyes. "Your father wanted to keep on wrestling but was denied. The dream for him to practice, compete, and who knows what else was taken away. But it looks different for you. You have an offer to join the team. I say you try. And if you like it, then learn to be good at it, like your father was."

Babak stood up and pushed the stool back beneath the bar. "But know that I am always proud of you. You are a good boy, a great student, and a blessing to the family. Wrestling or no wrestling, it does not matter to me as long as you are happy."

"Thank you, Uncle," Aarash said.

"Your father," Uncle Babak added, "would also be proud of you. I'm sure he and your mother are proud of you and watch over you every day."

Aarash stood up from his seat and looked at his uncle. "Thank you for telling me," he said with a smile. "I'll give it a shot. No promises though."

"Fine," Babak responded. "But there is one promise that I do want you to make this evening. Please don't tell Ferhana that I, as they say, spilled the beans about what you kids talked about today."

He paused. "It's good when a daughter can call her father and talk about her day. And you know Ferhana cares for you, don't you?"

"I know," Aarash answered. "I won't spill the beans to Ferhana," he jokingly added. "The team will meet on Wednesday after school. I'll let you know how it goes."

"That sounds good to me," Babak replied. "Now let's go home before your aunt scolds me for keeping you out so late."

CHAPTER 3

SIGN-UP DAY

Aarash and Anton were the first to arrive at the gymnasium. The hardwood floor—normally the basketball court—was covered by thick mats. They connected to form large, gold-colored circles.

"What are the circles?" Aarash asked.

"That's where you face off against your opponent," Anton answered. "Each one is ten feet in diameter. During a match, there will also be a larger outer circle. You have to stay within that during your match."

Anton moved toward the corner of the gym. He motioned for Aarash to follow him through a half-opened door leading to the boy's locker room.

"Come," said Anton. "I'll give you a quick tour before Coach starts the meeting."

Aarash grimaced as he entered the room. The combined pungent odor of sweat and cleaning products was intense.

Anton noticed Aarash's face and laughed. "I know, right? This is my third year here, and I still haven't gotten used to the smell of the locker room. I would say to crack a window open, but there are none."

"The coaches' offices are over there," Anton said, pointing beyond the lockers. "There's also a weight room on the far side of the gym. We'll spend a lot of time there—if you decide to join the team."

"Sounds cool," said Aarash.

They moved back out to the gym, where more boys had gathered. Coach Beckett was also there. He was tall and stocky and carried a clipboard. A pair of glasses and a whistle hung around his neck. Brown hair poked out of the sides of his baseball cap.

"It's go time," said Anton. "Hurry. Let's take a spot around the mats."

Aarash sat beside Anton and crossed his legs. He scanned the room but stopped quickly. Shane was also there and looking straight at him.

Aarash looked down. "Great," he quietly mumbled. If he joined the team, he might have to actually wrestle Shane.

"It's all good," Anton whispered, seeing Aarash's distress. "You'll be fine. Just relax."

Despite his friend's words, Aarash wasn't so sure. *Do I still have time to leave?* he wondered. *Being here will just give Shane the opportunity to mess with me some more.*

Coach Beckett reached for his whistle and blew a quick blast. "Settle down, gentlemen," he said. "It's time to get started." The room grew instantly quiet.

Too late, Aarash realized. He couldn't sneak out now.

"I count twenty-one of you here," Coach Beckett boomed, "including a lot of new faces. And believe me when I say I wish all of you would participate in this sport, but odds are that some of you will decide differently. And that's okay, because this team will demand a lot from you."

The coach paused and looked around at each boy individually. "I," he continued, pointing a thumb to his chest, "will demand a lot from you. I'm not asking you to be the best. I'm just asking for your one-hundred-percent commitment to the sport and to the team."

All eyes were focused on Coach Beckett. "Today's meeting will be simple," he said. He lifted his clipboard, and the pen tied to it dangled below. "I'm going to pass this around and have you each write your name, age, weight, and email. I'll send out a practice schedule and keep you posted on upcoming competitions."

Aarash nodded, along with the other boys. That seemed easy enough. But Coach Beckett wasn't done.

"I want you to see this team as a class," the coach said. "You will have homework, exercises, and reading material related to this wonderful and ancient sport so very rich in history."

Aarash heard a few disappointed sighs.

"Let's get started," Coach Beckett said.

The coach proceeded to call out the names of the varsity team members who were in attendance. Anton was one of them.

"Don't go anywhere," Anton whispered to Aarash. He walked onto the mat and took his place with three other wrestlers.

"These four outstanding young men have been part of the team since their freshman year," Coach Beckett said. "They will demonstrate some of the moves you'll learn in the coming weeks. Pay very close attention. You'll be on this mat, practicing your own takedowns, before you know it."

For the first demonstration, Coach Beckett had Anton and another boy named Javier enter the golden circle. Both boys leaned forward with outstretched arms. Anton's right hand cupped the back of Javier's neck. His other arm was lowered to his side. Javier had one hand behind Anton's neck and the other hand on his shoulder.

In a matter of a few seconds, Anton forced Javier's head down, then quickly released the pressure, forcing Javier to snap his head back up. Anton quickly moved in on his opponent and tucked his head into Javier's chest. With both hands now behind Javier's legs, Anton forced him to fall on his back.

"Takedown!" called one of the boys watching the demonstration.

"Double-leg takedown to be precise," responded Coach Beckett. He thanked his two wrestlers, then turned back to the rest of the group. "What you just saw showed stance, collar tie, a snap-down set-up, and above all, timing."

For the next half hour, Aarash and the other boys in the room watched as Anton and his teammates took turns pairing up and demonstrating different offensive and defensive moves. After each takedown, the coach went over the motions, as well as the dos and don'ts of the moves.

Aarash paid close attention and studied the different steps and combinations. He listened as Coach called out the two-point takedowns and reversals and the one-point escapes and penalties. He watched as Anton and the others showed a variety of locks, sweeps, and throws.

Through it all, Aarash thought about his father completing these same moves at his age. Thinking about it made him miss his father, but it was also a comforting thought. They had something in common, even if his father was no longer there.

At that moment, Aarash made up his mind. Even if it meant dealing with Shane, he was joining the team.

CHAPTER 4

PAIN WEEK

Aarash walked through the front door of his house a few days later. He had just finished working out with Anton and was drenched in sweat. His entire body ached, and Pain Week—five days designed to test physical endurance and commitment—was set to begin the next day.

Anton had been thrilled to hear that Aarash wanted to be on the team and had volunteered to spend the next few days showing him the ropes. Little did Aarash know that "showing him the ropes" meant endless drills and hours spent scrimmaging each day.

Maybe I overdid it, Aarash thought as he took off his sneakers and shuffled to the kitchen. *Maybe I'll be too sore to even do any of tomorrow's exercises.*

"Hey!" said Ferhana. She snuck up behind her cousin just as he reached for the jug of water. "You better not be drinking from the pitcher. That's gross!"

"I knew you were there," lied Aarash. "Besides, I only drink out of the milk container."

"Yuck!" Ferhana made a face as she grabbed a chair and sat with Aarash at the kitchen table. "Is Anton done training you?"

"Yup. I'm done. He's all yours," Aarash answered. "Tomorrow is the beginning of Pain Week, and I need to get some rest."

Aarash slowly got up. His muscles ached. His body was not used to so much exercise. He'd used muscles this week that he never knew he had—not to mention the running.

Why do we need to run so much? Aarash thought as he headed for the stairs to his room. *There's no running in wrestling!*

"You know," Ferhana called after him, "the week usually begins on Sunday. So you might be in Pain Week right now and not even know it."

Aarash was too tired to reply, but as he limped up the stairs, he thought, *Ferhana is probably right.*

* * *

The Monday of Pain Week consisted of running drills. The gym bleachers, which had been retracted on sign-up day, were now open and stretched ten rows deep and high.

The team spent the first ten minutes stretching. Then Coach Beckett had half the boys sprint up and down the bleachers. The other half was sent to run sprints across the basketball court. After twenty minutes, the two sets of boys swapped drills.

The next twenty minutes were spent hopping from one end of the gym to the other. After that, they had twenty minutes of jumping rope.

Aarash was exhausted. He could tell by the faces of the other boys that they were worn out as well. With the exception of a few dirty looks—and calling Aarash "A-Rash" whenever there was an opportunity—even Shane seemed too tired to be much of a problem.

At least for now, Aarash thought.

The rest of the week was a blur. Tuesday's drills consisted of push-ups, sit-ups, and jumping jacks. There was also a hopping exercise—designed to build lower-body strength—that required the boys to bounce across the gym with their arms outstretched above their heads. Once again, the last twenty minutes were spent jumping rope.

I wonder if my father was any better at jump rope than I am, Aarash thought as he tripped on the rope.

On Wednesday, Coach gave out twenty-five-pound weight plates. He showed the tired wrestlers how to hold the weights against their chests. Then he split the boys into two groups.

"I want to see one group sprinting up and down the bleachers and the other group doing laps around the basketball court," Coach Beckett said. "And make sure to keep those weights tight against your chests."

For the last drill of the day, the team dropped the weight plates and moved on to an activity Coach Beckett called "karaokes." Aarash skipped from left to right, moving his right leg over his left and following with his left leg over his right.

"At least we're not still hugging a cast-iron weight plate," he muttered to Anton as he tried to keep up.

"Don't jinx us," Anton responded, visibly out of breath.

Thursday saw much of the same. The drills continued with more bleacher sprints, push-ups, and burpees. There were also box jumps and high-knee skipping designed to build on speed and agility. The only difference from previous days was when Coach

Beckett sent the team outside to run ten laps around the school.

"Aren't you happy I had you running last week?" Anton joked as he ran next to Aarash. "Good thing I didn't let your complaining get to me."

"Yeah, sure," Aarash answered breathlessly.

"You can thank me later!" Anton responded as he picked up speed. He ran ahead, waving goodbye to his friend.

On Friday, Coach Beckett put out the same mats from sign-up day. After everyone had completed fifty push-ups, sit-ups, and burpees each, Javier demonstrated leg-work drills and wrestling stances.

Hunched forward, eyes on an invisible opponent, each wrestler mimicked Javier's moves. Aarash tapped his right foot, like Javier showed them, and clumsily stepped forward with the other boys until they reached the end of the mat. Once there, they turned around and repeated the process over and over again.

I wonder if this is how cavemen walked thousands of years ago before they decided to stand upright, Aarash thought to himself.

After Javier's demonstration was over, the team moved on to twenty minutes of high-knee extensions. It was similar to the previous day's high-knee skipping drill, only with more visible leg kicking.

At least this drill lets us stand upright, Aarash thought.

On his third lap around the gym, Aarash caught up with Anton. The older boy was also clearly out of breath.

"How do you go through this every year?" Aarash asked. "I'm exhausted."

Anton wiped the sweat from his brow and smiled. "Try not to think about it and focus on the end goal," he answered. "This is where you decide whether you really want to wrestle and be part of the team. Coach wants to see your commitment."

Aarash nodded in response. He would do his best—one drill at a time.

The day ended with fifty more push-ups and sit-ups and a stare-down from Shane that even Anton got a glimpse of.

"It looks like all this working out hasn't helped that guy's anger issues, has it?" Anton asked.

"Doesn't look like it," replied Aarash.

"He's probably just mad you're doing so well and keeping up with everyone else. Maybe he expected you to quit," Anton said. "Good for you for stepping up."

"More like sticking around than stepping up," Aarash added with a smile. "Now all I need to do is finish this last drill without breaking an ankle. I do *not* want to get benched with an injury on the last day of Pain Week."

CHAPTER 5

KNEE-JERK REACTION

At four-thirty on Friday afternoon, Coach Beckett blew the whistle. The sound officially marked the end of Pain Week.

A collective exhale echoed around the room. Out of the twenty-one students who had signed up for the wrestling team, only sixteen remained.

Aarash was more than ready for a break as he made his way home. Thankfully the weekend allowed for some much-needed rest and helped recharge his batteries.

When Monday arrived, Aarash was eager and ready to train. He felt refreshed and ready for his first official day as a wrestler.

"Congratulations on working hard and showing your commitment to the team," Coach Beckett began when everyone was seated on the mats. "Those of you who made it through, I'm glad to have you. I'd like to start our first official practice by telling you a little of the history behind wrestling."

Aarash was surprised. This was not what he expecting to learn on his first official day on the team.

"Wrestling started as a combat sport," Coach Beckett said as he began his unexpected lecture. "The Egyptians and Babylonians wrestled thousands of years ago. The ancient Greeks had wrestling competitions in the very first Olympics. For us, wrestling, or more precisely, folkstyle wrestling, will be a sport of rules and discipline."

"What's *folkstyle* mean?" someone behind Aarash asked.

"It's the form of wrestling that most high schools and colleges practice," Coach Beckett explained. "It's about having control on the mat, escaping your opponent's holds, and pinning him with both shoulders down on the mat. That's how you win."

"Don't worry. I'll show you winning, Coach," Shane interrupted from where he sat sprawled out on the gym's hardwood floor. The room erupted in laughter.

"Don't get me wrong," Coach Beckett said, stepping up to Shane. "I love it when we win. If you look at the hanging banners and trophy cases, you will see that the Freemont Pioneers have done a lot of winning. Winning will happen as long as we practice, stay disciplined, and learn."

Coach Beckett waited until Shane nodded. Then he turned to face the rest of the team.

"But there is more to winning," Coach continued. "There is teamwork—working together and learning from one another. There is knowledge—what you will learn about yourself, the sport, and each other. And there is grace—the fluid moves and motions, and more importantly, the dignity you display when you win or lose a match."

"This might be more than I signed up for," joked one wrestler.

"We'll see about that," Coach Beckett replied with a grin. "Now, let's get down to business. Today we wrestle!"

* * *

Aarash shook his head in disbelief. He could not believe his bad luck. Of all the people on the team, Coach had assigned Shane as Aarash's sparring partner.

Why did I ever listen to Anton? Aarash thought as he moved to the mat. *I went through that whole week avoiding Shane just so he could publicly humiliate me. Why me?*

Beads of sweat started to appear on his brow. He wanted to leave the mat, leave the gym, and avoid the whole situation.

"Geez," Shane said as he faced Aarash. "I haven't lifted a finger yet, and you're already sweating."

Aarash looked down and tried to swallow his fear. *If skills can be inherited*, he thought, *now would be a good time for those wrestling moves to kick in.*

But another voice also chimed in, telling Aarash to relax. He had worked hard with Anton before Pain Week. They'd even scrimmaged a few times in Anton's backyard during some of their after-school workouts.

I must have picked up something, *right?* Aarash thought.

Taking a deep breath, he got into position. Aarash replayed Anton's double-leg takedown from sign-up day as he waited for Coach to blow the whistle and start the bout. *Collar tie, downward pressure, release, step in, forward push, leg grab, takedown . . .*

Tweet! Coach blew the whistle.

Aarash crouched down, moved his hand behind Shane's neck, and applied downward pressure. Just as he released his hold and moved in to grab the back of Shane's legs, Shane kneed him in the forehead—hard.

Aarash dropped to the ground, and Coach Beckett blew his whistle again. Anton quickly moved in to check on his dazed friend.

"I'm sorry, Coach," Shane said as he stepped back off the mat. "It was a knee-jerk reaction." Sounding completely insincere, he added, "I'm sorry, A-Rash."

Aarash felt dizzy. "It's okay, Coach," he said as he tried to stand up. "He got me on the top of my head. The really hard part."

Aarash tried his best to make light of the situation. He didn't want to make things worse—or look weak in front of the team. What if Coach thought he couldn't handle himself on the mat?

Coach shot Shane an unhappy look, clearly irritated at the fake apology. "You sure you're okay, son?" he asked Aarash.

"I'm fine," replied Aarash. "Good thing it's just the first day of practice. I obviously have a lot to learn."

"Yes," Coach Beckett responded. "We *all* have a lot to learn, so let's begin by learning what *not* to do."

For the rest of practice, Coach went over the moves that were not allowed in wrestling. Anton and Javier demonstrated illegal and dangerous holds, including biting, kicking, punching, and choke holds.

Aarash half-heartedly watched the demonstrations. Once in a while, he looked over to Shane, who spent more time talking to the boy next to him than paying attention. Luckily, Coach Beckett was paying attention as well.

"Would you like to go to the mat and assist with the demonstration of illegal moves, Shane?" the coach asked.

"No, sir," Shane responded. He flushed, embarrassed at the reprimand.

"Then pay attention and learn how to *really* wrestle," Coach Beckett said firmly. "If it weren't for your knee-jerk reaction, I have no doubt your opponent would have succeeded in taking you down. At least he tried to execute a legal move."

Aarash appreciated Coach Beckett's clear support. He was also happy to see Shane looking uncomfortable for once. It wasn't exactly the win Aarash wanted, but it was still a win—of sorts.

CHAPTER 6

A HERO'S LESSON

On Friday, Aarash's first week as a member of the Freemont Pioneers wrestling team was drawing to a close. The week had been a combination of drills, practice, and lessons. Each day's lesson focused on two things: a position and a move.

On Monday it had been neutral position, sprawl defense, and basic single-leg and double-leg takedowns. On Tuesday, the team had learned about offensive top position and riding. Wednesday had been defensive bottom position and reversals.

And Thursday had focused on escape techniques, including hand control and hip heisting.

Through it all, Shane had continued to taunt Aarash, although he was careful to only do it when Coach was out of earshot. Thankfully, the rest of the team didn't seem to be finding Shane's "A-Rash" nickname very funny. Aarash only hoped Shane would grow tired of the mocking sooner rather than later.

At least everyone at home was proud of him. Ferhana had even surprised Aarash with a gift: headgear to protect his ears during practice and matches.

"It's cushioned," Ferhana said with a warm smile when she'd handed him the gear. "To protect your ears in case they get boxed in or pulled. It's also brand new and cleaner than whatever you've been using at practice."

As an added bonus, the headgear helped muffle most of Shane's insults.

Uncle Babak and Aunt Emily had also given Aarash a gift—a pair of blue wrestling shoes. The shoes were soft, snug, and comfortable. They even matched his new singlet—the official team uniform.

Aarash was feeling confident when he arrived at practice Friday. It started like every other practice that week. The team warmed up and stretched for the first ten minutes. This was followed with two drills covering what they learned in the previous days.

The first drill was the sprawl. Aarash and his teammates stood with their feet shoulder-width apart and knees slightly bent. With both hands extended and palms out, they hit the mat. They landed with their legs behind them, palms and upper body sprawled flat. Then they pushed up and landed back on their feet before repeating the motions again.

The second drill was a combination of square and staggered stances. Each team moved around the circle mats, changing stances every time Coach blew his whistle. The drill lasted for fifteen minutes and was followed by ten minutes of strength exercises: sit-ups, push-ups, and pull-ups.

Aarash was exhausted. His legs ached. The palms of his hands and wrists were sore from hitting the mat during the sprawl drills. His quadriceps were burning from dancing around the small wrestling circle practicing stances. Sweat soaked his T-shirt and matted his dark hair against his forehead.

Aarash felt a wave of relief as Coach Beckett blew the whistle, ending the final set of push-ups. He took a big gulp from his water bottle and sat on the mat between Javier and Anton.

While the boys caught their breath, Coach Beckett opened a folding chair. He set it in the middle of the half-circle formed by the team.

"Today's lesson will be different," Coach Beckett began. "We have a special guest. He's a former student from Freemont Central High. He was also a star wrestler for the Pioneers. Today, he serves as a lance corporal in the U.S. Army."

Coach Beckett turned and pointed to a uniformed man walking into the gym. "He is also," he continued with a smile, "my kid brother. I would like to introduce you to Lance Corporal Daniel Beckett, U.S. Army, Fortieth Infantry Division."

Aarash noticed the resemblance to the coach immediately. Both men were similar in height and build, but unlike Coach Beckett's curly brown hair, Lance Corporal Beckett had a military buzz cut. He also walked with a slight limp.

After greeting his brother, Lance Corporal Beckett sat down on the chair and faced the team. "Happy Friday, boys," he started. "From the look of you all, it's clear that the coach has been working you hard." He turned and winked at Coach Beckett.

"I'm here today to talk about the upcoming Tri-County Veterans' Memorial Tournament," Lance Corporal Beckett continued. "The purpose is to raise money and help support wounded soldiers and their families. It's also to honor the men and women who serve this country. I'm happy that Freemont Central has agreed to participate, and I look forward to seeing you boys compete in November."

Aarash and his teammates listened while Lance Corporal Beckett talked about his time as a Pioneer wrestler. They also learned he'd been an All-American in college and had planned to try out for the Olympics.

Ultimately, though, the lance corporal had decided that serving his country in the military was more important. When his patrol was attacked in Afghanistan, he'd been injured. His dreams of going to the Olympics had disappeared.

"I still got a medal," Lance Corporal Beckett told them. "And some metal." He bent down and lifted up his right pant leg to reveal a dark-gray prosthetic.

Aarash was surprised by the reveal. Even with the slight limp, he never would have guessed that Lance Corporal Beckett had actually lost a leg.

"He has your people to thank for that," whispered a voice from behind.

Aarash quickly turned and stared right into Shane's eyes. He couldn't believe what he'd heard. This insult bothered him more than anything else Shane had done or said before.

Picking on him in biology class, making fun of him in the hallways, the spitballs in the lunchroom, the knee to the head—these were nothing compared to what Shane was implying. These were accusations against Aarash's family. His uncle, his cousin . . . his father.

Picking up on the disturbance, Coach Beckett looked toward Aarash. "What's happening over there?" he asked.

"I heard everything loud and clear, Coach," Javier, who was sitting next to Shane, answered. "Shane just blamed Lance Corporal Beckett's injury on Aarash's family." He shook his head in disgust. "That's cold."

Shane looked up, his mouth hanging open, but nothing came out. He seemed shocked Javier had called him out.

"Why would you say that?" Lance Corporal Beckett asked, directing his question to Shane.

Aarash was still facing his bully, but he could see that Shane was now the one who was scared. And maybe not only scared. There was something else in his eyes. Was it confusion? Embarrassment? Maybe even shame?

"I'm sorry, sir. I didn't mean for you to hear it," Shane replied.

"Well then why did you say it to your teammate in the first place?" Lance Corporal Beckett asked.

"Because Aarash is from Afghanistan," Shane muttered.

Aarash turned back to face Coach Beckett and the lance corporal. He was furious at Shane and embarrassed to be in this situation. He looked down and focused on the laces of his shoes.

"Aarash?" Lance Corporal Beckett asked. "That's a strong name. It means 'first ray of the sun,' correct?"

"Yes," Aarash responded, still looking down.

"You should be proud of your heritage, Aarash," the lance corporal said. "I hope your teammates—even the one behind you—make an effort to learn about your culture."

"I'm sorry, Lance Corporal Beckett," Shane said. "I—"

"Don't apologize to me. Apologize to Aarash," Lance Corporal Beckett interrupted. "He's your teammate. He's the person you should support. Working together is important. Learning from each other is important, no matter how different you think you are."

Coach Beckett stepped forward and gave the wrestlers a hard look. "I couldn't agree more. If anybody here can't get behind these simple aspects of being a team, then you should reconsider being here," he added. "I don't want to waste your time, and I don't want you to waste the team's time."

The room was quiet. Aarash could hear and feel the blood pulsing in his ears. He felt a hand on his right shoulder. It was Javier. Another teammate placed a hand on his left shoulder. Aarash turned and saw it was Jack Eng, another freshman wrestler.

After a moment, Lance Corporal Beckett continued his talk. Aarash looked up and nodded at the two teammates by his side. From the corner of his eye, he saw Anton give him a smile and a thumbs-up.

Aarash shifted and stayed seated. Nobody got up to leave that Friday—not even Shane.

CHAPTER 7

AWAY MATCH

Three weeks had passed since Lance Corporal Beckett had come to practice to talk about the Tri-County Veterans' Memorial Tournament. Since then, the Pioneers had been practicing and training for their first meet of the season against the North Valley Lions. This would be Aarash's first official bout as a wrestler.

Aarash was excited, eager, and a bit nervous to go up against his North Valley opponent. He fiddled with the tie on his hooded sweatshirt as he looked out the window of the team bus.

He wished Anton was with him today to help calm his nerves. But Anton had been sidelined because of an injury playing basketball with friends the weekend before.

Too bad, Aarash thought. *The team could have really used him today. And I could have used the support.*

Luckily, Shane didn't seem too interested in Aarash—for once. He sat at the back of the bus and kept to himself.

Maybe he has the pre-match butterflies too, Aarash thought.

"Hey, Ray." One of his teammates tried to get Aarash's attention. "Ray?"

Aarash turned to face Jack. Since Lance Corporal Beckett's visit, some of the guys had taken to calling Aarash "Ray," a loose translation of his Pashto name.

Aarash didn't mind the nickname—it was cool. It made him feel like part of the team.

Besides, he thought, *it sure beats "A-Rash."*

"You weigh yourself this morning?" Jack asked.

Aarash nodded. The officials would weigh all the wrestlers before the competition began. They would be divided into groups and matched with opponents based on their weights. But Aarash had wanted to have some idea where he'd be grouped.

"I was around one twenty-seven or one twenty-eight," he answered.

"I weighed in at one thirty-nine," Jack responded. "I hope my bathroom scale is right."

"We'll find out in a bit," answered Aarash as the bus pulled into the North Valley High School parking area.

From the outside, North Valley High looked brand new. But once Aarash entered the gym, the newness of the school disappeared. Everything seemed standard. Even the locker room had the same aroma of sweat and chemicals that Aarash was now familiar with.

There were around forty spectators sitting in the bleachers—mostly parents, siblings, and friends.

Aarash was excited to see his uncle, aunt, and Ferhana waving at him from their seats. There was also a surprise—Anton was with them. He gave Aarash a thumbs-up.

Looks like I'll have plenty of support after all, Aarash thought, waving back.

The teams gathered for the official weigh-in before the matches began. To Aarash's surprise, he came in at one twenty-five, placing him in the one-twenty-six weight class.

I need to get a better scale for the house, Aarash thought to himself.

Once the weigh-in was finished, the Pioneers grouped together on one side of the gym. The Lions were on the opposite side. The teams were separated by a black mat with inner and outer circles both outlined in red. That was where the competing wrestlers would face each other.

The gym buzzed with excitement. Aarash could hear chatter from every direction. That came to an end as soon as the announcer called for everyone's attention. The referee stepped on the mat, and the announcer called up the first wrestlers.

"First up we have Aarash Husayni versus Claudio Martinez for the one-hundred-twenty-six-pound junior varsity weight class," he said.

Aarash secured his headgear and stepped into the inner circle. He shook his opponent's hand, and the referee blew the whistle to start the match.

Each wrestler locked on. Aarash had one hand on Claudio's shoulder and another on his wrist. The two wrestlers circled the inner ring, struggling for control. Aarash's mind raced to find an opportunity to bring his opponent down, but everything was chaotic. There was no plan.

Aarash felt Claudio tug on his headgear, then break, take a step back, and lunge forward with both knees on the ground. Aarash was dragged down with him as Claudio locked both arms around Aarash's right leg for a single-leg takedown.

Aarash twisted his body on the floor, attempting to break free. He ultimately broke from the hold, wrapped his arm around his opponent's waist, and tried to flip Claudio.

But Claudio fought back, reversing his position. He knelt behind Aarash and forced him flat on his stomach.

For Aarash, the match felt like an eternity. In reality, it was no more than a few minutes until he finally pushed himself off the ground, turning his opponent over. Aarash used his full force to pin both of Claudio's shoulders to the floor for the required two seconds.

The buzzer rang, and both competitors returned to the inner circle to shake hands. The referee then stepped in and raised Aarash's arm, declaring him the victor.

It was Aarash's first bout—*and* his first win! He could hear the roars of support from his teammates. He could also make out the joyful cheers from Ferhana, who wildly waved from the bleachers.

Aarash's heart raced and his face froze in a huge smile. *Winning,* he thought, *feels awesome.*

But the biggest shock came from Shane. He congratulated Aarash as he joined the rest of the Pioneers.

"Not bad for your first match," Shane said coolly. "You took him down fast. Right in the first period too."

"It didn't feel fast," Aarash answered. He was still winded from the match.

"Well, looks like I'm up," Shane said as the announcer called the next pair of wrestlers to the mat for the one-hundred thirty-eight pound match. "Tasovac versus Belcastro. Wish me luck, Aarash."

"Good luck," Aarash automatically responded.

But as Shane walked away, Aarash was confused. *Did Shane really mean the compliment? He's never called me by my actual name before. What changed?*

CHAPTER 8

WHY WRESTLING?

News of Saturday's win was broadcast throughout the school during homeroom on Monday morning:

"The Freemont Pioneers wrestling team took the win over the North Valley Lions! Let's congratulate freshmen Aarash Husayni, Shane Tasovac, and Jack Eng for their first-match wins, as well as our seasoned wrestlers, Javier Guzman, Brendon Pugh, and Nick Pappas. The final score was 41–27."

For the first time since coming to Freemont Central High, Aarash felt good. *Really good*. He walked the halls with an extra bounce in his step. Anton had been right. Wrestling *was* good for him. Aarash only wished his father had been in the bleachers watching him during Saturday's competition.

That afternoon, Coach Beckett congratulated the team as a whole. He didn't call out the wrestlers who'd won or lost their individual matches. Instead, he noted that he was proud of everyone's conduct and how they'd supported one another as a team.

"It's been a little over a month, gentlemen," Coach Beckett said after the team broke from drills, "and I'm happy to see improvement and growth. You are acting like a team. You're behaving like athletes should behave. And you're learning from one another."

Aarash knew Coach was right. The team had grown more disciplined. It seemed that everyone, even Shane, took the drills and practice seriously.

"Today," the coach said, "we'll be doing things differently. I want us to learn more about each other. I want us to talk. We can pick up on wrestling moves and positions again tomorrow. But today we will take a break from the physical work and concentrate on getting to know one another."

"I'd rather do the push-ups," Javier joked quietly to Aarash.

"I won't make this too difficult," Coach continued. "Let's call today's lesson 'Why do you want to be a wrestler?' Sound good?"

A number of the boys nodded their heads in agreement. Aarash did too. He didn't mind taking a break from the drills. He was still sore from the meet.

"Great, I'll help break the ice and start," Coach Beckett offered. "It's simple. I wanted to be a wrestler because my father was a wrestler. My brother had the same reason, more or less. He wanted to become a wrestler because I was a wrestler. Like I said— simple."

Coach Beckett scanned the room and stopped at Javier. "Guzman. Why did you join the wrestling team?"

"My answer is simple too, Coach," Javier started. "I wanted to become a wrestler because nobody in my family wrestles. They prefer soccer."

Coach Beckett smiled. "Fair enough," he said. "How about you, Shane?"

Shane looked surprised. "Um, can you ask someone else, Coach? My reason is lame."

"There is no lame reason," Coach Beckett insisted. "All reasons are valid."

"Okay," Shane started. "If you really want to know, my stepdad suggested I join the team. I've always played team sports like football and baseball, but he thought the individual competition that you get in wrestling would be good for me. You know, when it's just you against one other person. That way the win or the loss—the mistakes—it all falls on you."

"Your stepdad sounds like a smart man, Tasovac," Coach Beckett said. "And he might be on to something, but rest assured, we are a team here."

Aarash scanned the room, wondering who the next person would be. To his surprise, Coach Beckett's eyes landed on him.

"How about you, Aarash?" Coach said. "Why wrestling?"

"Anton made him join," Javier called out before Aarash had the chance to speak.

Aarash nodded. "That's partly true. Without Anton I would never have joined the team, but I also joined for another reason."

Aarash realized that the room had grown quiet. He took a moment to collect his thoughts before he continued.

"Like you, Coach, my father wrestled. But I never knew that. I only found out from my uncle shortly before I joined the team. Turns out my dad was a high school wrestler, but that ended when the Taliban took over Afghanistan," Aarash continued.

"I hope your father is proud that you've followed in his footsteps," Coach Beckett answered.

Aarash looked down, twirling his shoelaces. "I don't know, Coach," he said. "He's not here anymore."

"What happened?" one wrestler asked. "Did the Taliban kill him?"

"Nope. It was a drunk driver," Aarash responded. "It happened when I was eight . . . only a few months after we moved to the United States. My dad was a translator for the U.S. Army back in Afghanistan. Because of that we were allowed to immigrate to America."

Coach Beckett moved closer to Aarash. "I'm sorry to hear about your father, Aarash," he said. "It sounds like he was a good man and lived an interesting life. I'm sure he's watching over you. And that he's proud of you."

"Thanks, Coach," Aarash answered, confident that his father was watching over him. "And I'm happy to be part of the team."

"Yeah, Ray!" one of his teammates cried out.

"Go, Pioneers!" called out another wrestler.

For the next half hour, each wrestler gave his reason for joining the team. Jack even confessed that he didn't know what he was getting into when he showed up for the sign-up meeting.

"I thought it was going to be like the professional wrestling on TV. I even picked out my wrestling name," Jack added proudly. "The Terminator."

Aarash and the rest of the team broke out in laughter. Even Coach Beckett joined in.

* * *

After practice, Aarash went to unlock his bicycle from the bike rack. Shane was waiting for him.

"What's up?" Aarash asked nervously. He wasn't sure where things stood with Shane. He was still surprised by what seemed to be a change in attitude since Saturday's meet. But he wasn't sure if it was genuine.

Best to keep my guard up, Aarash thought to himself.

"I've been doing a lot of thinking, and I've been meaning to talk to you," Shane started. He took a few steps closer to Aarash. "I get it. The team. The way they interact with you. It's made me see how I've been treating you. I'm a jerk. Hopefully I *was* a jerk—past tense," he corrected himself.

"Yeah, you were," Aarash agreed. "Why? What did I ever do to you?"

"Honestly, nothing really," Shane responded. "You were just . . . different. Or at least I assumed you were. I'd love to give you a good reason for the way I acted—like my father was killed fighting terrorists or something—but that would be a lie."

Shane paused and looked down. "The truth is," he continued, "my dad isn't exactly a nice person. Especially not to people who aren't like him."

For the first time Aarash wondered what Shane's personal life was like. "So what changed?" he asked, surprised by the honesty.

"My stepdad," Shane replied. "He's been trying to help me. That's why he suggested I join the team. Meet new people and make friends. I'm not doing so well on the making friends part."

He's got that right, Aarash thought.

"Coach Beckett and his brother also made me realize that the way I've been treating you is not how a teammate acts," Shane said. "And it's not who I want to be. I mean, we're all different, but as a team, I don't know. I guess we're the same. We're all Pioneers."

He looked at Aarash nervously. "I just want to say I'm sorry. I know it doesn't erase how I've acted, but I'm trying to do better. I hope you'll accept me as your teammate."

Aarash thought for a minute. Shane was right. The apology didn't erase everything, but it helped him understand Shane a bit more. And in his heart, Aarash knew his father would be forgiving.

"You're right. You and I—we're Pioneers," he said. "We're cool."

"Thanks, man," Shane answered, offering his hand to Aarash. "We're Pioneers! And we are going to dominate in the veterans' tournament—as a team."

"Definitely," replied Aarash. "As long as you quit calling me 'A-Rash.' You can call me 'Ray.' That nickname's kinda starting to grow on me."

"If you don't mind, I'd rather call you 'Aarash,'" Shane answered. "I actually think it sounds cooler."

Aarash nodded in approval. If Shane was willing to try, he was willing to give him a chance.

CHAPTER 9

TOURNAMENT DAY

It was the day of the Tri-County Veterans' Memorial Tournament. Three weeks had passed since the team's first meet against the North Valley Lions.

Although Aarash and the other freshmen had limited experience facing challengers from other schools, they had worked hard these past few weeks. Besides, win or lose, they all knew that today's event was for a good cause—raising money for veterans in need.

"There's lots of competition out there," Aarash said as he scanned the other teams assembled in the athletic center of Mission College. In all, there were nine teams in the tournament.

"Looks like an all-day event," Anton agreed.

Aarash was amazed at the size of the complex. There were hundreds of spectators. Like last time, Ferhana and Aunt Emily were in attendance and sitting in the stands. But there was no sign of Uncle Babak.

He's probably at the restaurant, Aarash assumed.

He felt a bit guilty that he wasn't able to help his uncle as much as he used to, but he knew Babak would rather have him involved with wrestling than busing dirty dishes.

"You remind me of your father when you talk about your practice and what you've learned," Uncle Babak had recently told Aarash. "This brings me joy and makes me think of happy times."

A scoreboard fixed on the wall behind the announcers' table displayed the rankings of all the different teams competing. The Freemont Pioneers were in third place, behind the Averill Cougars and the Carmel Sea Wolves.

Luckily, the results wouldn't affect the school rankings, since this was a charity event. Not all eligible teams were participating.

A military band played the national anthem to help kick off the event, and then it was time to wrestle. Aarash faced off against his first opponent, but he wasn't used to wrestling in the offensive starting position, which placed him on top of his opponent. He quickly lost control. The other wrestler gained the upper hand in a reversal and pinned Aarash to the mat.

Though disappointed, Aarash told himself it was fine. At least he felt more confident and able to execute a greater variety of moves. And this was a double-elimination tournament, meaning he still had a chance. In fact, he couldn't wait to get back on the mat.

* * *

It didn't take long before Aarash was back on the mat and facing off against a wrestler from the Averill Cougars. They shook hands, and the referee blew the whistle marking the start of the match.

Although his opponent matched Aarash in weight, he was slightly taller and more powerfully built. Aarash could feel the vice-grip strength of his rival's holds and his intensity as he tried to force Aarash down.

Aarash pushed his opponent's right hand off his arm. He quickly moved behind, grabbing his rival by the waist and dropping him to the mat, gaining two points for the takedown.

Clearly upset, the Cougar swung his forearm to break Aarash's hold and struck him on the side of his head. The referee took note of the unnecessary roughness. He gave Aarash one more point and blew the whistle to mark the end of the first period.

Momentarily shaken by the unexpected hit, Aarash went back to the inner circle for the second period. This time he would take the defensive, or bottom, starting position. His opponent would be behind him with one arm wrapped around Aarash's waist.

The whistle blew, and Aarash quickly escaped the hold, gaining one more point. But it didn't take long for the Cougar to gain control again. He lifted Aarash and brought him to the ground in a near fall. This gave the Cougar two points.

Aarash struggled as he tried to keep his shoulders off the mat to avoid getting pinned and losing the match. He tried kicking himself up and managed to break from the hold on the second try. His opponent momentarily lost his balance, giving Aarash an opening to reverse the hold and gain the upper hand.

Unfortunately, his attempt to pin his opponent came to a sudden halt when the referee blew the whistle. That was the end of the second period.

Both wrestlers were exhausted as they entered the circle to begin the third period. Aarash was winded and struggled to catch his breath. This time, Aarash had the offensive position. He could hear his opponent's heavy breathing and knew he had two minutes left to win the match.

The whistle blew again. Aarash used all his strength in an attempt to force the Cougar off-balance for the pin. But he wasn't quite strong enough. The Cougar pushed up off the ground, forcing Aarash to his side.

Aarash quickly pushed up before his rival could gain stability and attached himself to his opponent's back. He wrapped one arm around the other boy, hooking his hand on the back of the other wrestler's neck.

The Cougar tried to shake Aarash off but to no avail. In a final burst of strength, Aarash forced his opponent to his back and gained a decisive victory with a match-winning pin.

The referee blew the whistle a final time and slapped the mat to indicate the pin. The two wrestlers shook hands, and the referee raised Aarash's left arm, declaring him the winner.

Aarash stepped off the mat, where he was greeted by his teammates. Anton, Javier, and Jack surrounded Aarash and patted him on the back.

"Impressive," said Anton. "You did really well out there."

"I think your win bumped us up to second," said Javier.

"That guy was tough," said Aarash. His legs were unsteady, and he felt the strain on his side. But he also felt pleased with himself.

"Great wrestling," said a voice from behind Aarash. "I could definitely learn a thing or two from you."

Aarash turned around and faced Shane. The former bully stretched out his arm and offered his right hand.

"So what do you think?" Shane asked. "We're doing okay as teammates. Is it too early to work on us becoming friends?"

Aarash accepted Shane's outstretched hand. "I'm willing to give it a try if you are," he replied.

CHAPTER 10

KEBABS AND KOFTAS

After a long day at the Tri-County Veterans' Memorial Tournament, the Freemont Pioneers finished in third place. In addition to placing in the top three, Aarash and the Pioneers came out of the event as a tighter team.

The day was full of surprises. After the results were announced, Aunt Emily approached Coach Beckett and spoke with him for a moment.

When she finished, Coach Beckett turned to the team.

"We're all invited to Aarash's family's restaurant to celebrate today's event," he said. "They were kind enough to extend the invitation to all the Pioneer family members attending the tournament today."

The team cheered and high-fived. They were starving after a long day of competing.

Outside, the sun was setting as the team drove to Babak's Kebab and Grill. On the bus, the wrestlers were more lively and energized than they'd been at the start of the day. Many were reliving the day's events and the matches they'd been in.

Aarash spent the first part of the ride joining in with his teammates and listening to the play-by-play action. Then he settled back in his seat and stared out at the sky. His muscles felt strained and sore. His hair was sticky with sweat that had now grown cold.

Slowly his mind wandered to a different part of the world and a different time. He wondered if his father had experienced the same thrill of competition and the togetherness of a team.

Maybe that's why he loved wrestling, Aarash thought. It was nice to imagine that they had that in common.

"Mind if I join you for the rest of the ride?" Lance Corporal Beckett stood in the aisle.

Aarash was surprised to find him there. "I didn't know you were riding with us."

"I was up front with Coach," the lance corporal answered. "Saw the empty seat next to you and wanted to come back to congratulate you on your performance."

"Sure thing," answered Aarash. "It's all yours!"

"Great," answered Lance Corporal Beckett. "I'm a little rusty on my Pashto. Hope you don't mind a quick refresher before I meet your uncle."

Aarash nodded with a smile. "Happy to help."

* * *

By seven o'clock, Babak's Kebab and Grill was bustling with activity. Uncle Babak had reserved the main dining room for the Pioneers and their families. Each table was crammed with platters of traditional Afghani foods, and the air was filled with a variety of savory aromas.

Aarash, Ferhana, Anton, Shane, Javier, and Jack sat together at a table. Ferhana took the lead and started passing around the dishes.

"This sure beats the school lunchroom," said Jack.

"By a mile!" responded Javier.

Coach Beckett stopped by the table just as Anton dropped a giant spoonful of mantu meat dumplings and kofta meatballs on his plate. He tried to balance them on the mound of rice he already had there.

"Great job today, boys," Coach Beckett said. "You all did very well, on the mat and off."

"Go, Pioneers!" Anton hollered, momentarily distracted from the food on his plate. The cheer was repeated several more times by others in the room.

"Try not to eat too much, Anton," Coach Beckett joked. "I don't need you going up a weight class."

"Don't worry, Coach, he's got a high metabolism," Ferhana said. "He also loves Afghani food. I think that's why he wanted to be friends."

At that moment Uncle Babak came by with a tray of meat dishes and set them on the table. "Our specialty," he exclaimed. "Lamb and chicken kebabs!"

Everyone at the table reached for the pita-wrapped meals—everyone but Shane. Aarash noticed Uncle Babak's surprised look.

"What's wrong?" Babak asked Shane. "Give it a try. You will love my kebabs."

Shane looked up apologetically. "I'm sure I would, but I'm a vegetarian," he responded.

Aarash smiled. He had a lot to learn about his new friend.

"Even better!" Uncle Babak said. He motioned to his wife, who was busy coordinating the dishes. "Emily! Please bring out a bowl of pumpkin-lentil soup, dolmas, and my special stuffed vegetable turnovers."

"So much for *any* of us making weight next week!" Aarash announced.

The boys burst out laughing. Aarash smiled as he looked around the table. He'd finally found something that had been missing for most of his life—a team to belong to and a tight group of friends he could depend on.

GLOSSARY

agility (uh-JIH-luh-tee)—the ability to move fast and easily

decisive (dih-SAHY-siv)—able to make choices quickly and confidently

diameter (dye-AM-uh-tur)—the length of a straight line through the center of a circle

endurance (in-DUHR-uhnts)—the ability to handle long periods of exercise

immigrate (IMM-uh-grate)—to come from one country to live permanently in another country

insincere (in-sin-SEER)—not expressing or showing true feelings

metabolism (muh-TAB-uh-liz-uhm)—the process of changing food into energy

prosthetic (pross-THET-ik)—an artificial part that takes the place of a body part, such as an arm or leg

pungent (PUHN-juhnt)—having a strong or sharp taste or smell

quadricep (KWAH-druh-sep)—a muscle in the front part of the thigh

reprimand (REP-rih-mand)—a severe and formal criticism

scrimmage (SKRIM-ij)—a practice game

valid (VAL-id)—fair or reasonable

veteran (VET-er-uhn)—a person who served in the armed forces

DISCUSSION QUESTIONS

1. Throughout the story, Aarash had the support of his friends, family, and teammates. Have you ever supported a friend or family member who was struggling with a difficult situation? Talk about the situation and what you did to help resolve it.

2. Aarash was surprised to learn that his father was a wrestler, but the discovery also motivated him to join his school's wrestling team. Have you ever been motivated to join a team or club because of a family member or friend's similar experience? Talk about the experience and what inspired you to learn something new.

3. Ferhana and Anton convinced Aarash to join the wrestling team, even though he was unsure in the beginning. Why do you think each of them wanted Aarash to join the team? Were their reasons the same or different?

WRITING PROMPTS

1. Imagine that you are Aarash and are debating joining the wrestling team. Write a list of pros and cons for each outcome to help you make your decision.

2. After Lance Corporal Beckett and Coach Beckett talk to the team, Shane apologies to Aarash. Try rewriting the end of Chapter 8 from Shane's point of view. What do you think he was thinking? Why do you think his behavior changed?

3. Throughout the story, Aarash thinks about his father and what he would do in similar situations. Imagine you are Aarash and write a letter to your father describing your experience on the wrestling team. What would you want him to know?

Wrestlers are divided into weight classes—groupings determined by weight. This is done in an effort to keep each bout—or match—fair and evenly matched. A wrestler needs to be on or below a specific weight in order to make weight at the time of the meet.

High school wrestlers compete in fourteen weight classes established by the National Federation of State High School Associations (NFHS). They include the following categories—106, 113, 120, 126, 132, 138, 145, 152, 160, 170, 182, 195, 220, and 285.

Wrestlers need the proper equipment. Basic gear includes:

- **headgear**—gear worn to protect the ears while wrestling
- **mouthguard**—protective gear used to protect a wrestler's teeth from injury
- **singlet**—a sleeveless, one-piece uniform worn by wrestlers

Here are some other moves, terms, and positions wrestlers should know:

- **All-American**—a wrestler who finishes in the top eight of his or her weight class in a national tournament
- **bout**—a match between two wrestlers consisting of three periods

- **collar tie**—a hold used by a wrestler to grab an opponent by the back of the neck
- **double-elimination**—when a wrestler must lose two bouts to get knocked out of the event
- **escape**—when a wrestler breaks from the control of his or her opponent and gets back on his or her feet, scoring a point
- **folkstyle**—the style of wrestling used in high schools
- **neutral**—the position wrestlers take at the start of a match, facing each other
- **offensive top**—when a wrestler is on top of or behind his or her opponent
- **penalty**—when a wrestler is awarded a point as a result of an opponent's violation
- **pin**—when a wrestler forces his or her opponent's shoulders to the mat, resulting in a win
- **reversal**—when a defensive player comes from underneath and takes control or returns to standing position
- **riding**—when a wrestler controls his or her opponent on the mat
- **sprawl defense**—a move used to counter an attempt by the opponent to grab the legs for a takedown
- **stance**—the position a wrestler takes during a match
- **takedown**—when a wrestler forces his or her opponent to the mat from a standing position

LOOKING FOR MORE
WRESTLING ACTION
THEN PICK UP . . .

JAKE MADDOX JV

HEAVYWEIGHT
TAKEDOWN